46,625

E
CAR   Carson, Jo

      You Hold Me and I'll Hold You

              V O I D

You Hold Me and I'll Hold You

STORY BY JO CARSON

PICTURES BY ANNIE CANNON

Orchard Books   New York

Orchard Books, 95 Madison Avenue, New York, NY 10016

Manufactured in the United States of America. Printed by General Offset Company, Inc.
Bound by Horowitz/Rae. Book design by Mina Greenstein.
The text of this book is set in 16 point Novarese Medium. The illustrations are watercolor,
tempera, colored pencil, and collage, reproduced in full color.
10 9 8 7 6 5 4 3

Library of Congress Cataloging-in-Publication Data
Carson, Jo, date. You hold me and I'll hold you / story by Jo Carson ; pictures by Annie
Cannon. p. cm. "A Richard Jackson book."
Summary: When a great-aunt dies, a young child finds comfort in being held and in holding,
too.   ISBN 0-531-05895-6. ISBN 0-531-08495-7 (lib. bdg.)
[1. Death—Fiction.] I. Cannon, Annie, ill. II. Title. PZ7.C2388Yo 1992
[E]—dc20 91-16370

To Heather and Mary
—J.C.

To Florence
—A.C.

WE WERE AT HOME. Daddy was cooking. Helen was watching TV.

I wanted to be watching TV, but I was supposed to be cleaning up my room. I'd put stuff under the bed already, but Daddy said that wasn't cleaning up, and then I got under the bed and Daddy got mad, so I was cleaning up my room really.

I hate cleaning up my room.

The phone rang, and I thought it might be for me, so I went to the kitchen, which I wasn't supposed to do because I hadn't finished cleaning my room, but I needed to know who was calling and if they wanted to talk to me.

They didn't. It was for Daddy.
He said, "Oh, no! I'm so sorry to hear it."

I didn't like that. I've been sorry to hear some things myself. My mother decided she couldn't live with us anymore and moved away. I don't like it when somebody says they are sorry to hear something.

It makes me wonder how sorry I'm going to have to get.

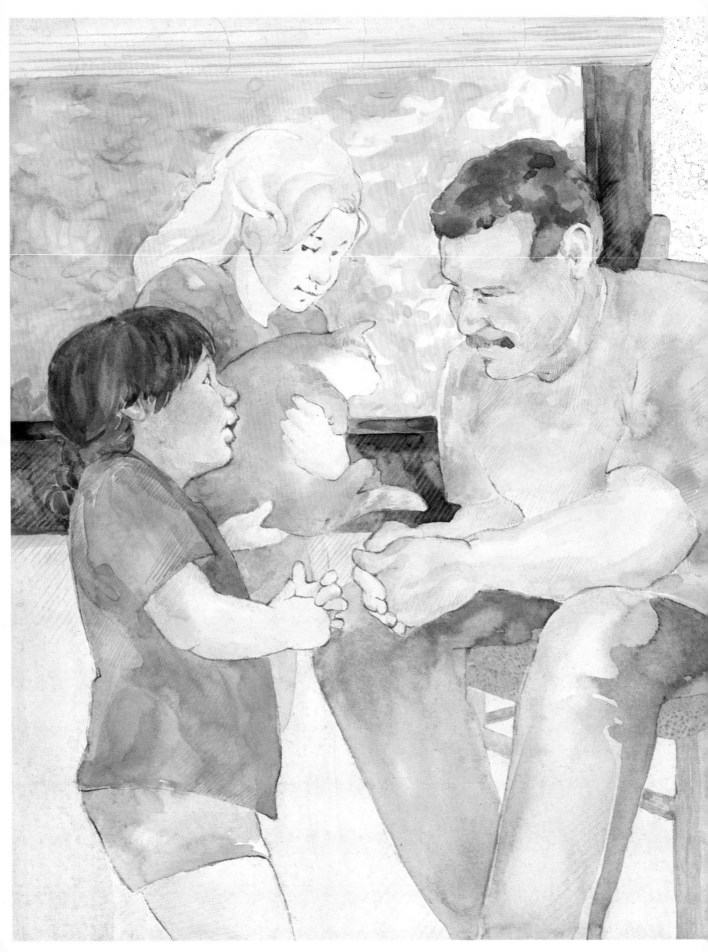

When Daddy hung up, he said we'd get in the car and drive to Tennessee. He said we'd take our Sunday clothes because we were going to a memorial service.

"What's a memorial service?"

"My Aunt Ann died," said Daddy. "We'll go to church for her tomorrow."

Then he asked if I had finished my room yet. And I asked what was going to happen if I hadn't, and he said it sounded to him like I better go back and work some more.

Died. A goldfish I knew died. We flushed him down the johnny.

Helen's hamster Henry died. His name was Henry Hamster. We buried him. I preached because Daddy said every funeral he'd ever been to had a preacher.

I said a poem I made up. Dig, dig, dig 'cause Henry died, died, died.

I piled some stuff I hadn't cleaned up yet on top of me to see what it felt like, except I could still hear the TV, and I was under it when Daddy came to see if I was through.

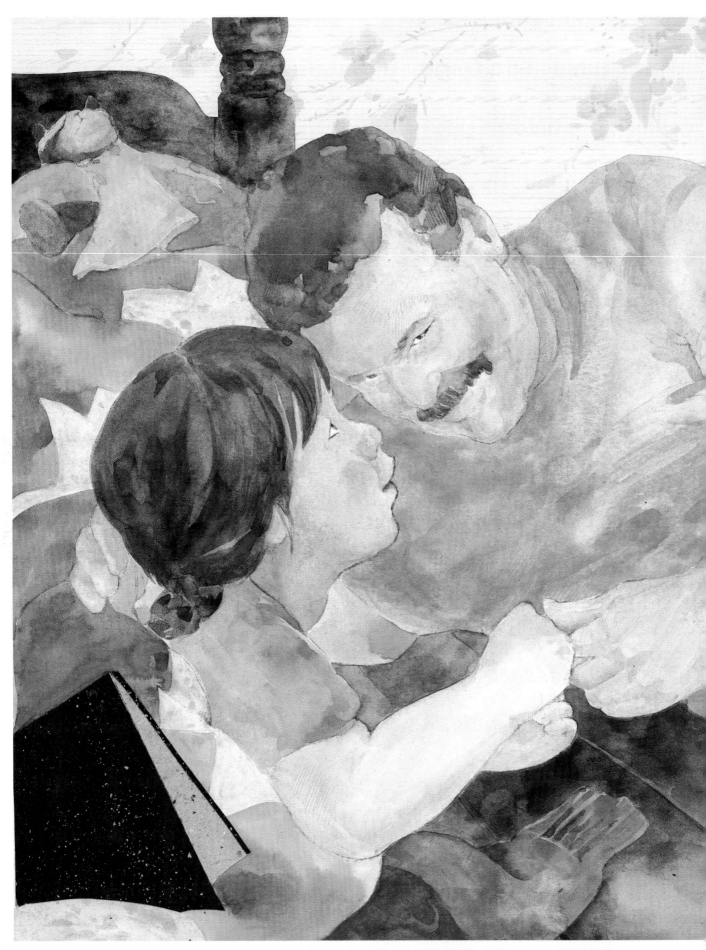

"Dig, dig, dig 'cause Henry died, died, died,"
I said.

He hugged me.

"You're thinking," he said. "I can hear the wheels turning."

"Will it be like Henry tomorrow?"

"Bigger. There will be lots of people."

"I'm not the preacher this time, am I?"

"No, but her preacher is probably working right now like you did for Henry."

"I did good for Henry."

"You sure did."

He made me finish my room whether I did good for Henry or not.

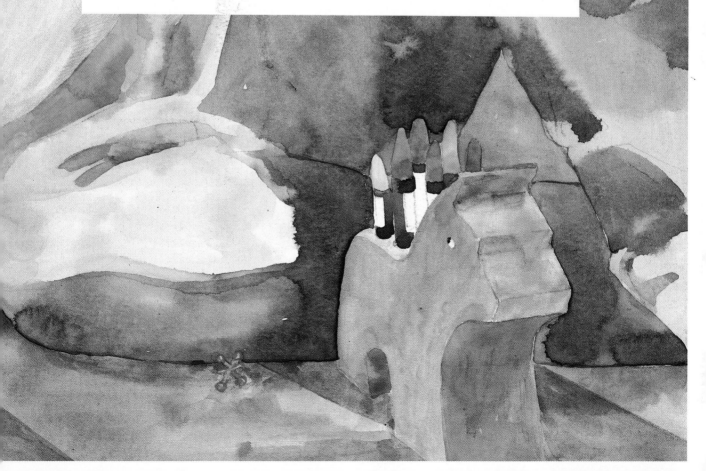

The next day we drove to Grandpa's house in Tennessee. Aunt Ann was his sister. Helen and I changed into our dresses.

Daddy tied a towel around my neck before I could eat lunch because he said people were going to be looking at me and I had to stay clean all the way down to my socks.

Helen had a towel tied around her neck too and Helen doesn't usually have to do what I have to do. She's older.

We went to a church. Grandpa and Grandma Jan went with us. Jan's not my real grandma, but she's just as good.

A person Daddy knew but I didn't said, "The family is in the chapel," and pointed down a hall. It didn't look like family to me. I didn't know anybody except Daddy and Helen and Jan and Grandpa.

People seemed to like me, though, so that part was okay.

Then everybody got in a line and went to the big room of the church and sat down all together. Jan was next to Grandpa, I was next to Jan, and Helen was next to me, and then Daddy. I'm getting to the hard part next.

The preacher was saying all the stuff he thought of, and I was going to tell Jan what I said for Henry, but when I looked at Jan, she was crying. I didn't know Jan ever cried.

And Grandpa was crying.

I looked at Daddy, and he was crying. Helen saw them too.

And I got the feeling that's wondering how sorry I have to get.

Jan asked if I wanted to be held, and I said yes, and she lifted me onto her lap. She whispered that it was all right to cry; it was a sad occasion.

She said, "You've been sad before too, haven't you?" And I said, yes, I had.

I was about to cry, and I make noise.

What I really wanted was for Daddy to hold me.

And he knew. He held out his arms, and I got in his lap, and he whispered, "You hold me and I'll hold you."

It was good to be held, and it was good to be holding too.

You hold me and I'll hold you. It's what I'm going to say if I ever have to preach at another funeral.

It made me feel better.